D1412189

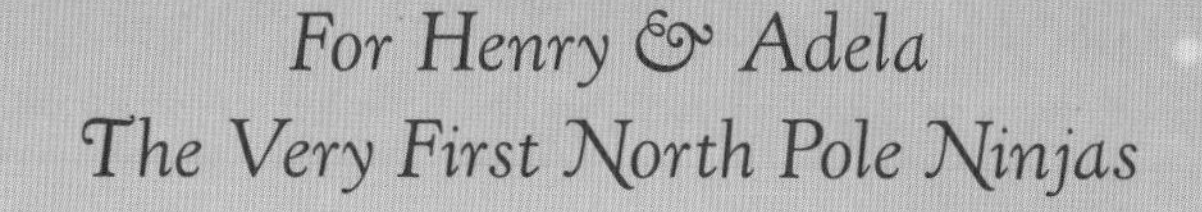

For Henry & Adela
The Very First North Pole Ninjas

PENGUIN WORKSHOP
Penguin Young Readers Group
An Imprint of Penguin Random House LLC

Penguin supports copyright. Copyright fuels creativity, encourages diverse voices, promotes free speech, and creates a vibrant culture. Thank you for buying an authorized edition of this book and for complying with copyright laws by not reproducing, scanning, or distributing any part of it in any form without permission. You are supporting writers and allowing Penguin to continue to publish books for every reader.

Text copyright © 2016 by Tyler Knott Gregson and Sarah Linden. Illustrations copyright © 2016 by Penguin Random House LLC. All rights reserved. First published in 2016 as part of the *North Pole Ninjas: Mission: Christmas!* box set by Grosset & Dunlap. This edition published in 2018 by Penguin Workshop, an imprint of Penguin Random House LLC, 345 Hudson Street, New York, New York 10014. PENGUIN and PENGUIN WORKSHOP are trademarks of Penguin Books Ltd, and the W colophon is a trademark of Penguin Random House LLC. Manufactured in China.

Library of Congress Cataloging-in-Publication Data is available.

ISBN 9781524790790 10 9 8 7 6 5 4 3 2 1

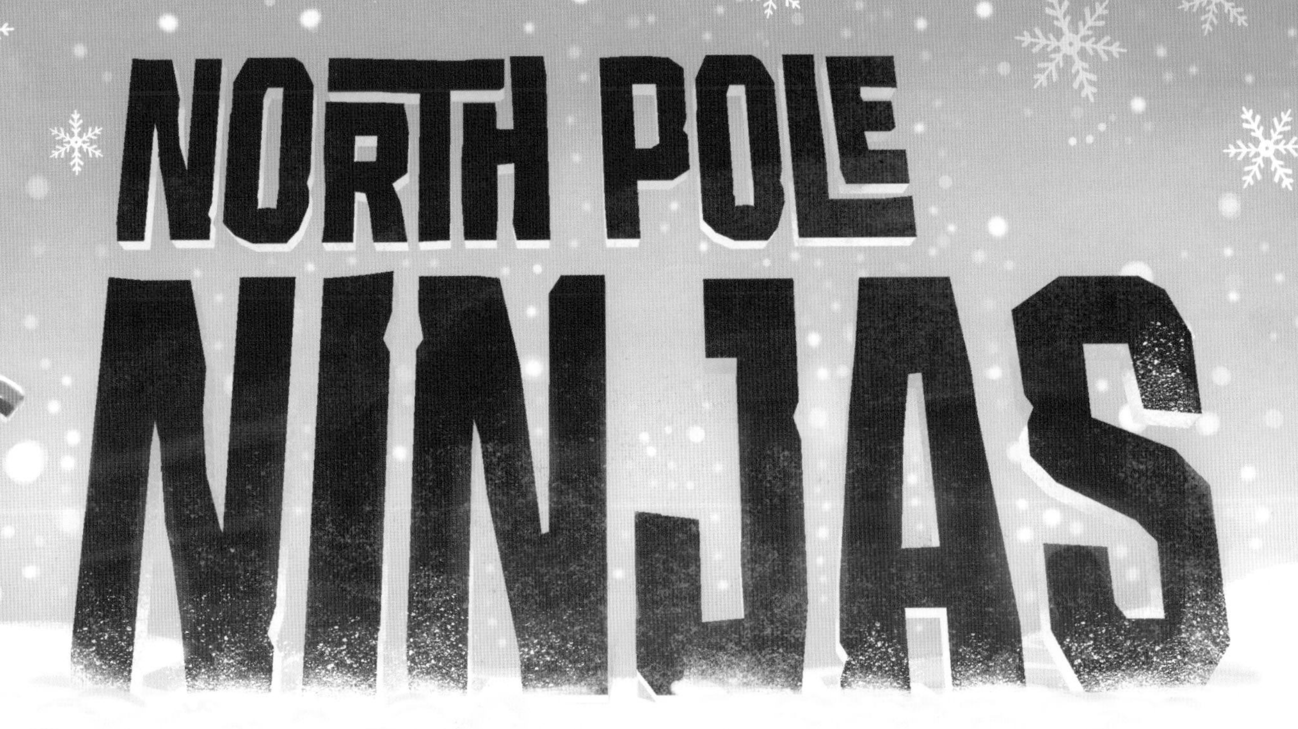

MISSION: CHRISTMAS!

BY TYLER KNOTT GREGSON & SARAH LINDEN
ART BY PIPER THIBODEAU

PENGUIN WORKSHOP
AN IMPRINT OF PENGUIN RANDOM HOUSE

There's a secret at the pole
that not too many know.

Long ago it was hidden
deep beneath drifts of snow.

We all know about the elves
who work in Santa's shop.

They stay busy all year round
and hardly ever stop.

There are elves who make the toys,
and those who feed the deer,
some who sprinkle the cookies,
one in the sleigh to steer.

But there are some secret elves
who are not often seen.
They spend their Christmas giving
in masks of red and green.

These are the North Pole Ninjas.
They live for Christmas Day.
They are masters of helping,
led by Santa's sensei.

He's tiny, round, and quick,
a beard right to his toes.
The teacher of the secrets,
or so the story goes.

And he is filled with magic,
much more than it may seem.
Santa is always thankful
these elves are on his team.

For it's these North Pole Ninjas
who always do good deeds.

They use their Christmas spirit
to care for others' needs.

These Ninja Elves are mighty.
When spreading their cheer around

with random acts of kindness,
they never make a sound.

It might not happen often
to elves so filled with care,

but sometimes this special team
has jobs it needs to share.

Santa gave them permission
to ask for help from you.

Consider yourself chosen!
Now you're a ninja, too!

So you must keep the secrets,
for you are on their team.

An honorary ninja,
more magic than you seem.

Stay hidden and stay quiet
when shoveling that snow.
Secretly you'll save Christmas,
no footprints where you go.

Now dig deep through your closets.
Find all that doesn't fit:
hats and coats, unworn sweaters,
skates or a baseball mitt.

Then peek around your kitchen
for treats you love to eat.
Donate sardines, soups, and beans.
Pack up the cans of meat.

So when you get a mission,
a job from your sensei,
tuck him inside your pocket,
and then be on your way.

Just know that Santa's grateful
and needs these elves the most.

He sees all the good you do.
There's never need to boast

Bring a bag of groceries to your
local food bank to share food
with those in need.
2
Write a letter to your
best friend telling them exactly
love them.
doorstep.
feel happy.

Now you're part of the secret.
Prepare yourself to act.
You and the North Pole Ninjas
have made a Christmas pact.

When Santa's bag is empty,
and reindeer start to soar,
you'll stay a North Pole Ninja—

now and forevermore!